COUS... LOVE!

Together in Every Way

Harris Sherman

Expressing our Gratitude!

Thank you for choosing "Cousin Love!"

Welcome to a world where cousins create magical memories together! This enchanting book beautifully captures the delightful bond cousins share, engaging in various activities through rhythmic storytelling. With its charming animal watercolor illustrations, it celebrates the special affection and joy that comes from having cousins by your side. This keepsake is a perfect reminder of the love, laughter, and unforgettable moments cousins bring into our lives.

If you and your little ones enjoy the journey these pages offer, we warmly invite you to share your reflections on Amazon.

Your feedback is invaluable in helping other parents discover this fun filled book and make informed decisions when gifting for their little ones' special occasions.

Thank you for your support!

To _____

from _____

When we meet, our hearts do race,
Tight hugs, a warm embrace.

Every time, it's pure delight,
Cousins make the world feel right!

Jumping high on trampoline springs,
We laugh as happiness sings.

Up we go, in joyful cheer,
Cousins' love is always near!

Out in the field with bats and balls,
We play till the evening falls.

Swinging bats, runs scored in fun,
Cousins' laughter shines like the sun!

With paints and brushes, colors bright,
Cousins create with sheer delight.

On canvas and clothes, our art does show,
Together, our colorful love does grow!

Rolling in grass, under skies so vast,
Cousins giggling, having a blast.

Green stains mark our fun today,
In this field, our love will stay!

Huddled close on movie night,
Cousins watch with thrill and fright.

Gripping hands, we dare not peep,
Shared scares make memories deep!

On scooters bright, we glide and soar,
We race fast, hearts galore.

With every twist and every turn,
Cousins' love, we always learn!

In the pool, we splash and swim,
Cousins laughing, full of vim.

Water fights in the bright sun's gleam,
Together, we make the perfect team!

Down the slide, we laugh and zoom,
Cousins together, our joy in bloom.

Hand in hand, we climb once more,
In the park, our spirits soar!

On safari, wild and grand,
We explore the animal land.

Through binoculars, we spot and cheer,
Cousins' love grows strong and clear!

On a blanket spread with treats,
Cousins gather, joy completes.

Sharing sandwiches, fruit, and cake,
Picnic bliss we lovingly make!

Pillows tossed in gleeful flight,
Cousins laugh into the night.

In the bedroom, joy's in bloom,
Laughter fills our cozy room!

On a road trip, miles we roam,
We make the car feel home.

Singing songs and sharing snacks,
Cousins' love fills every track!

Grinning wide with gaps so neat,
Cousins show their missing teeth.

Laughter shared as we compare,
In this moment, joy we wear!

Ghostly games in dim-lit halls,
Cousins scare with playful calls.

Shrieks and giggles, spooky fun,
Fright and laughter, all in one!

On the beach, sand castles rise,
Cousins craft under sunny skies.

Moats and towers, built with joy,
Seaside fun, our best employ!

With bedsheets, tents we create,
Magic of togetherness, oh so great.

Under our fort, we laugh and shout,
Cousins' love on a night out!

A Loving Note for You

Capture the MOMENT

Selfie

Thank You!

Did you find delight in the vibrant journey within our book, "Cousin Love!"?

If the imaginative adventure in our book touched your heart and you believe it makes the perfect gift for your kids and their cousins, we would be incredibly grateful for your feedback in the form of a review on Amazon.

Your valuable insights do more than just support our small business; they also help other families discover the magic and joy within this vibrant book. Reviews like yours ensure that more children can experience the warmth and excitement of our stories.

To explore a broader selection of captivating books, visit the "Harris Sherman" Author page on Amazon. Your support means the world to us,

Wishing you cherished moments with your little cousin!

Warm regards,

Harris Sherman

Made in United States
Troutdale, OR
10/30/2024